AF487903

Infinity, Infinity, and a Palm Tree

BY THE SAME AUTHOR

FICTION

Infinity, Infinity, and a Palm Tree (novelette)

2024–Big Sister Is Watching You
– coming in 2027-28 (novelette)

NON-FICTION

No Dramas–7 Short Stories about Coming of Age during the
Fall of a Superpower
– coming in March 2025

Does the White Crow Belong to the Cuckoo's Nest?
– coming in 2026-27 (memoir)

FOR YOUNG ADULTS

Does Your Mother Know?
– coming in 2025-26

Infinity, Infinity, and a Palm Tree

A STORY OF LOVE, LIFETIME AFTER LIFETIME

Clara White

White Crow Publishing, LLC
San Francisco, CA

Copyright © 2024 by Clara White
All rights reserved. No part of this publication can be reproduced, distributed, or transmitted in any form or by any means, including photocopying, recording, or other electronic or mechanical methods, without the prior written permission of the publisher.

For permission requests, email the author, subject: "Attention: Permission Request," at the website clarawhitewriter.com

Printed in the United States of America
First Printing, 2024

ISBN (paperback): 979-8-9916372-0-6
ISBN (eBook): 979-8-9916372-1-3

Book design and production by www.AuthorSuccess.com

WARNING!

Please use your own senses to filter the furnished information to align with your own beliefs, experiences, and knowledge.

DEDICATION

To Freddie Mercury, who inspired me to reach for the stars and to "wear my heart like a crown" proudly.

Contents

You look into his eyes—you see yourself for the first time.
You hold his hand—you feel safe and protected from all
elements.
You hug him—you discover that you have found your way back
home—you are not lost anymore.
You kiss him—your world is expanding and melting into
something new.
He made it into your reality in this life.

—The White Crow

Infinity, Infinity, and a Palm Tree

Prologue

FROM LARA

Do you believe in love at first sight? I used to, but now I am aware of the true nature of this phenomenon. It is not falling for someone new on the spot—it is recognizing a loved one from your past life.

Time slows down, and the world seems to fall away. Your hands are sweaty and shaking, and you want to burst into tears. You feel your heart in your throat, beating too loud and too fast, and you desperately need to touch this person to accept that they are for real.

Now, here is the "onion" (a metaphor for a story with multiple layers that need to be peeled away to get to the heart of it): that is how my future husband felt when he saw me for the first time. He looked like he had been struck by lightning or had seen a ghost, and he is not even the spiritual one in our family.

****

After observing several of my past and future lives, I finally understand the mechanics of being reincarnated: possessing the same soul every time, but always (understandably) given a different body, and (surprisingly) a different spirit to help you achieve your potential. I am grateful to my current life's Spirit for carrying me through all my heartbreaks, disappointments, and obstacles; for not allowing me to give up on myself; for bringing into my life so many amazingly beautiful (inside and out) people who help me or accept my help; and for giving me the opportunity to survive, stay positive, and feel loved just for being me!

I

My past life regression mediator's soothing voice brings me back to reality from flying in the sky: "Lara, let us move forward today in one of your future lives. What can you see now?"

There is a magnificent lake . . . I stayed here with Alex and Rachel a couple of years ago. It is Lake Como, with a floating stage in the middle of its "Y." There are multiple levitating platforms around it with seated people wearing stylish, comfortable clothing in muted colors. They are facing the stage and the timeless view of the mountains behind it. A big crowd is collecting on the shore. They are drinking their refreshments from strangely shaped small bottles.

It is the middle of summer—a hot, humid night. The stage is illuminated with pinkish lights that make you feel cool. Their soft glow is coming from above, but I cannot see its source.

There is a group of more than a dozen musicians with different instruments on the stage, including Scottish bagpipes, Ukrainian long flutes, acoustic and electric guitars, drums of all shapes and sizes, and the Jewish Violins of Hope.

A man in his twenties comes out of nowhere, holding the hand of a young woman. She looks tiny and fragile next to him. Her makeup-free face has a lot of personality. You would not describe her as a classical beauty, but somehow her face is totally stunning, framed by a wavy mop of dark hair. The man lets go of her hand, making her look momentarily lost.

He is striking, with short, curly, dark blond hair; huge, smiley, confident steel-gray eyes; and the lean body of a warrior. He moves on the stage with athletic ease. He is not aware of the power of his appearance, or maybe he just does not care. The girl is his singing partner and has developed an emotional attachment to him. So, he needs to tread carefully, keeping his distance but showing respect for her feelings. She has a huge voice full of modulation, power, and pain that creates a stark contrast with her small frame.

I am looking down at this young man's soft loafers from inside now. OMG—I am him!

As if this realization were not enough, I catch sight of a man with smoldering eyes in the front row, staring at me. I cannot believe he came to our concert! Those eyes, with so much intensity and fire in them, belong to one of the professors from the University of Milan—UNIMI—who interviewed me this winter for the Dottorato di Ricerca (Ph.D.) in astrophysics. I am still on their waitlist. The man portrays their motto, "Scientia illuminans dignum," so well, being a recipient of the Nobel Prize for establishing a connection between dark matter and the non-biological energetic matter that all of us carry inside.

"We are performing today to raise money for natural habitats that have been badly damaged by war," says the announcer. "Wildfires are still raging there . . ."

The first song is my adaptation of Queen's "The Show Must Go On." I called it "The Fight Must Go On." By substituting just a few words and sentences, I completely changed the meaning of the song, switching the focus of attention from one man's broken heart and approaching death to the struggle of an entire nation, addressing the world in its quest for freedom. Freddie would be proud! It must be the end of the twenty-first century if this song's copyright has expired.

Let me show you what I did with the chorus part, completely rewriting the lyrics for it:

THE FIGHT MUST GO ON!
MY HEART INSIDE IS BREAKING,
MY HOPES ARE BADLY SHAKEN,
BUT MY SPIRIT STAYS STRONG!
THE FIGHT MUST GO ON!

"Lara, can you tell me more about yourself in this life, please?"

Sure, I see myself now in one of my houses. It is a modern green structure that mixes well with its surroundings. Inside, everything can be operated by my voice. There is a huge piano that looks like a pipe organ with floating monitors in the middle of the room; this piano can read the melody from my mind and play it back to me. The sound quality is fantastic. The floor-to-ceiling windows on one side of the house look out at the majestic lake. I am a decent singer who writes mostly adaptations of famous rock songs from years past. I want to bring these raw talents back to life. I am financially sound, doing it for different charities that support the causes I feel passionate about.

I also teach quantum physics in a small high school for gifted youth in Florence, Italy. I like working half days for nine months of the year with long summer breaks; it makes me feel like a kid who never left school. I have bought and completely renovated a place that used to be a Renaissance artist's studio during the time of the Medici. When I had a couple of walls removed, I found a treasure hidden within one of them—a helmeted image of the most celebrated Florentine beauty of the Renaissance, painted on a tournament banner. I feel a strong connection to the place and to this painting. I will miss all of it terribly when I move to Milan for my Ph.D.

I am happily gay with strong sapiosexual tendencies (attraction to intelligence). I have not found a life partner yet—brainy guys can be dry (and I mean it—VERY dry), or needy in a pessimistic way, or annoying (often late to everything, and apologizing constantly without any intention of ever changing their behavior), or completely hopeless at organizing their life affairs. My household consists of a very efficient middle-aged woman, who is my personal secretary, and two Siamese cats, who are their own "people."

I want to have a child and a dog one day, but they would require the stability of unconditional love from two joyfully married people. Being old-fashioned, I believe we all need happy parental figures present during the very formative time of our childhood. I am sure that the right person will find me at the proper time.

"Lara, was your childhood a happy one?"

Definitely. I have fond memories of weekend outings, celebrations, long vacations, concerts, theatre performances, quiet family evenings spent reading books and playing games, and hugs and kisses before bedtime for me and my younger brother. Our parents are patient, kind, generous, and intelligent people who know how to enjoy their life together.

II

Once a month, less often if I am lucky, I wake up shaken to the core, ice cold, with painfully clenched teeth. My dreams take me from the comfort of my warm, cozy bed, which I share with my husband Alex and our dog Rocky, snoring in unison; from the safety of our lovely townhouse in San Francisco with our teen daughter Rachel, tucked in her bed next door . . .

I am back in the USSR, in the family I was born into. In my nightmare, I have just seen myself as a thirteen-year-old, spending a weekend with my father, who is heavily drunk, as usual. My mom is in the hospital.

I go to our tiny kitchen to get a glass of water to keep next to my bed for the night and pass my dad. He is completely wasted.

"Would you like a glass of water from the kitchen, Daddy?" I ask in a small voice, trying not to sound scared.

"And who are you? Who let you into my apartment?"

I see madness in his eyes that makes me shrink inside from the fear of being beaten again.

"Ah, you finally found me! I am going to kill at least one of you before you take me!" Father rants.

He runs into the kitchen surprisingly fast, then catches me

at our front door, desperately trying to escape the apartment. He is holding me from behind, a knife to my throat. I am afraid to make any sharp movements. The only thing I can do now is grab the blade and slowly push the knife away. Pain, blood, blissful darkness . . .

In the morning, Father says that he bandaged my hand after I had hurt myself. Now he wants to take me to the doctor instead of school.

He tells me, "You should be grateful that I was able to stop the bleeding, saving your precious pinky after you cut it to the bone." I realize that he does not remember what really happened. I feel numb inside.

Throughout his entire life, my father was afraid of being arrested by the KGB as a grandchild of an "Enemy of the State." I learned about his family's past only after his death at the end of *perestroika*, which was a process of restructuring the economic and political systems in the former Soviet Union.

The next day, I go to school for my first class, physics, my favorite. I spent the last couple of months getting ready for a major contest between the middle schools in our town. Physics is easy for me with all the formulas and functions I learn every day. I can see the objects from my textbook's problems drifting in my mind and can calculate the results of their movements, predict trajectories, and explain the outcomes. It feels so light, so dependable; it is difficult to explain how much satisfaction and validation it gives me when our teacher says, "And now, here is another extra difficult problem for Lara to solve today."

This time around, though, I am staring hopelessly at the problem in front of me. There is no light and no movement; the air is still. I feel tears collecting in my eyes. I cannot understand what is being asked of me. The magic is gone!

I run from the classroom without asking for permission to leave.

Heavy drinking was all too common in the gray brutality of Soviet life, and my physics teacher had seen plenty of abused kids in her long career. A brief look at my bruised wrists and my damaged pinky, and she knew why her favorite student's eyes, usually bright and curious, were now lifeless. She never called on me again to solve any extra difficult problems. Her kind face will be imprinted in my mind for the rest of my life.

Since that night with my father, I have had periodic blackouts. Sometimes, I cannot be a hundred percent sure if some episode has happened to me in real life or not, because my mind has a habit of going completely blank. This makes me feel like Alice in Wonderland; I never know what kind of scare will trigger my fall into a hole again, usually ending in a panic attack.

****

One of my past lives

I hear my mediator's voice coming through the fog of my mildly hypnotized brain. "Lara, let's move with the poles of light carrying you to one of your previous lives. What can you see?"

Everything is out of focus . . . I see myself on a sandy beach wearing a white tunic and high-top sandals. I am boarding a beautiful ship that looks like it could have come straight from the pages of the Greek mythology books I loved to read in my childhood. I am a young warrior who joined this regiment a month ago. We are leaving for our first battle after being in training for the last couple of years.

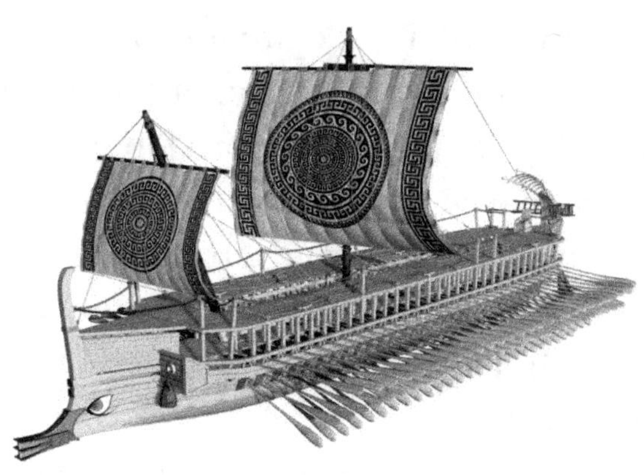

We are ancient Greek soldiers—hoplites—from relatively wealthy families that have provided us with our own armor and weapons. Our army is called the Athenian Hoplite. My mates are constantly joking about our commander being hot for me; I feel his eyes following me all the time. I have curly, light-chestnut hair, big steel-gray eyes (from my mother, an African slave),

and a lean light brown body with still developing muscles. I am kind and always take our unfinished food down for the slaves who row our ship.

Our commander is a strong, stoic, well-respected man in his early thirties. I can recognize Alex in him—sometimes, he shakes his head from side to side in the same manner to clear his thoughts.

I am summoned to his space at the ship's bow in the middle of a quiet, tender night. We are drinking wine and talking about tomorrow's battle when he suddenly takes my hand and starts slowly covering my palm with gentle kisses. I feel confused, but as he continues moving up to my arm, then my shoulder blade, an overwhelming sense of tranquility replaces my fears—maybe he has added something to my wine. He is an amazing lover who gives more than he takes (definitely Alex). He does not want to do anything to hurt me, but wants to feel one with me . . .

The next day, I kill my first man. I catch him by surprise from behind before cutting his throat. He had the hazel eyes and sad disappointed smirk of my current life's father.

"Okay, let's get you out of the battle to see what you were doing later in this life, and whether you had a family."

Moving forward, I see myself as an aging man with a severely damaged knee wrapped tight in a brown leather brace. I am an instructor for youth, living at a military school headquarters. I love poetry and philosophy, and those are the subjects I teach the future hoplites. On my days off, I go to see two prostitutes, one woman is my age, the other is slightly younger. I treat them well.

I know that I was gravely wounded in my first battle, and that our commander was killed in it, while blocking a sword's swing that was aiming to finish me off. He fell on top of me along with the dead body of an enemy. I was saved once again by a slave at the end of the fray. He paddled to the shore, dragging me with him; then remained my friend and serf for the rest of my life, even though I set him free. I see myself dying, and he is holding my hand.

He is crying, calling me "master."

"Lara, what did you learn from this life?"

"I discovered that I do not want to be a warrior again. I would like to know how it feels to bring more beauty into this world instead of destroying it."

III

Back to my current life

In my twenties, after the 1993 coup in Moscow ended the people's hope for freedom and democracy, I decided to leave Russia. I was badly depressed after seeing dead bodies right in the center of the city.

At the beginning of October 1993, a power struggle between President Boris Yeltsin and the Russian Parliament after the dissolution of the Russian Congress created a constitutional crisis. This is how another bloody "October Revolution" started in Moscow on the second day of that month, bringing thousands of angry people to the city streets. They came to protest the deteriorating living conditions and the inability of the current government to resolve the escalating situation of unpaid salaries, organized crime, and empty supermarket shelves. The protestors wanted the impeachment of the president, whose use of the police force led to the killing and wounding of hundreds of people who showed their support for the Russian Parliament. It all ended with the shelling of the House of Parliament, on the early morning of October 4, by the tanks of the Russian army that sided with President Yeltsin.

DEEP SADNESS

(written in October of 1993; translated into English in 2022)

There is a big city in a vast country
In a nation that is cursed.
Its people are doomed;
Their spirits are broken when they are born.
This metropolis has a lot of electric lights and traffic.
There is a darkness of night with a full moon,
A full moon every day.
It's the color of blood.
The city is very old—almost 900 years.
It has seen a lot of despair from regimes and warfare.
There is a tall building somewhere within.
It has a small flat with a view of the burg.
One girl likes sitting on a windowsill,
Where she loves to dream.
Her fantasies are about becoming a bird:
A white crow that breaks free from her black flock.
This girl knows that she has food and a roof overhead.
There are plenty of good friends in her life.
She needs to be grateful and happy,
But her heart is full of sadness.

Deep, deep sadness
She cannot explain.
The city is brimming with military parades and people without smiles.
There are so many beautiful churches,
But there is no God.
The Lord's divine presence
Was taken from their hearts.
The girl used to laugh,
But now her mind is full of sadness.
Deep, deep sadness
She cannot explain.
Something is missing,
But what?
She wants to feel safe and loved,
But she doesn't know how, because she has seen too much blood,
So many broken and wasted lives.
After all those parades, there is always another coup or war.
Violence consumes young people's beautiful bodies:
Flesh that had dreams and hopes,
Minds that were full of curiosity and life.
The girl is fed up with empty promises,
She wants to throw up.
This one is not afraid of death anymore,
But she fears the power of love.
She does not want to lose herself in it.
The young woman knows about sex,
About its mechanical part.
It feels hard and violent.
She dreams about just being hugged.
The girl's body is full of sadness.
Deep, deep sadness

She cannot explain.
Her hope is waking up one day
To the glory of the morning sun,
In the warmth of an embrace that will make her feel safe,
Safe and satisfied.
Is it too much to ask for?
Her soul is full of sadness.
Deep, deep sadness
She cannot explain.

It is impossible to unsee other people's pain and death. It stays in your mind and heart for the rest of your life. It took me more than four years to open myself to new beginnings. But life always gives you a rope to pull yourself out of any difficult situation, if and when you are ready to accept help.

IV

**April 1998: A comedy theater night with my friend
Tatiana Repina**

Ms. Repina was an extremely attractive woman in her late forties. My older friend was intelligent and well-educated, the only daughter of a former KGB general. My nickname for her was Rep.

The theater's box office did not have any tickets left for the show. Three drunks were trying to sell Tatiana their passes so that they could buy another bottle of vodka. They wanted money for all three tickets at once. Traditionally, a bottle of vodka was shared between three people (something to do with a special glass for it). Rep had enough cash to buy only two passes from them. That's why she ended up stopping strangers, trying to persuade someone to buy the third one.

Alex was a passerby who could not leave a lady in distress, and he agreed to pay for the spare ticket.

I was running late for the show because it was Tatiana's turn to get us in. When I arrived at the theater, she was standing in front of the entrance with a good-looking guy. I thought it was another victim of my charismatic friend, who was habitually spoiled by men's attention. This stranger turned pale after staring at me for several long seconds and excused himself to go inside.

All three seats were together, with Tatiana's in the middle. Alex and I were constantly laughing at the same jokes during the show. Rep had a different sense of humor, and gave us looks from time to time that said, "Really?" The play featured several aging movie stars and was a total intellectual entertainment dream come true.

I felt uncomfortable about Alex's Ukrainian accent, which I could hear clearly when he addressed Tatiana. I did not want her to get in trouble with this much younger man who could hurt her pride. I had already gotten two proposals for a fake marriage from guys who wanted to get permission to live in Moscow. Being a Muscovite was like being an American; you had to be born there or get married to one to stay for a prolonged period. I came back from the powder room during intermission and caught my friend giving Alex my phone number.

"Tatiana, do you think we could talk for a moment, please?" I was trying to keep my voice under control.

"Oh, dear, there is really nothing to talk about. Alex lives in America."

"I do not care where he lives . . ."

"And he is inviting us to a very nice restaurant after the show," Rep interrupted, as usual.

"Apologies, I need to talk to her in private," I said to Alex, since I was not having any success with Tatiana. He stepped aside.

"Rep, do you have enough money left for a fancy dinner? Because I do not, and I still owe you for my ticket." (At that time, only foreigners or wealthy Russians had credit cards.)

"Nonsense! A man who invites a woman for a meal pays for it."

"Ah, but I am not used to letting a man I just met pick up the tab. So, the two of you go ahead, and enjoy the rest of the evening."

Alex appeared behind me. "It is truly not a big deal for me to pay for dinner for all three of us, and it will make my last evening in Moscow complete if you agree to join us."

At the steakhouse, Tatiana ordered the most expensive dish with a glass of wine, while I went with salad and water. Alex could not take his eyes off me, and his hands were shaking slightly. As a result, he spilled a full glass of water on my lap. Good thing I was wearing a leather skirt that evening. I reached for Rep's half-empty wine glass.

It was late by the time we were done with dinner. Then, Alex wanted to take us all the way to Tatiana's front door. I usually stayed at her downtown flat if it was too late to go home.

Rep whispered in my ear on the way to her apartment, "All men are the same, bastards! Watch, now he is going to ask to come up for a nightcap."

Alex said good night in front of her building, asked for permission to call me in the future, and kissed my hand before leaving us (me deeply shocked by this old-fashioned gesture).

Tatiana looked at me with triumph. "Impolite bastard! He did not even try to have tea with us!"

I loved my friend, her unorthodox sense of humor, her bright and bubbly personality, and her undying optimism. Later, she would follow me all the way to New York City, bringing with her our practice of going to the shows every Friday night, this time on Broadway, and taking turns buying tickets at the 49th Street discounted box office at Times Square.

****

Middle of July 1998

After almost three months of nightly calls from New York City, Alex was coming back to Moscow. I had never laughed that much in my entire life, talking about nothing and everything. We were finishing each other's sentences during those calls while exchanging our coming-of-age stories. We even brought some humor into our painfully awkward first times. By the end of the second month, I felt comfortable sharing with him every thought that came into my head. It was like slowly recognizing someone I had known forever, someone from whom I had been separated all this time. I could breathe fully again, feeling grateful for being alive and so deeply connected to another human being.

We planned a trip to spend ten days together—half the time in Moscow, the rest in Budapest. Alex made the arrangements for both of us. He had always wanted to see Hungary, and now he also set his mind on showing it to me.

Upon Alex's arrival from Sheremetyevo Airport, we spent the entire day walking the streets of Moscow, carrying his small travel bag. We ended up being caught in a terrible rainstorm after he was done faxing something for his work from the business office of the Danilovskaya Hotel, of all places. It was surrounded by several Russian Orthodox churches, cathedrals, and a couple of monasteries.

The oldest structure of all was the Svyato-Danilov Monastery, which was initially built in the late thirteenth century by one of the sons of Prince Alexander Nevsky. It was rebuilt several times and had a very dark history of being used as a prison for youth whose parents were executed as "Enemies of the State" during Stalin's regime. This monastery was returned to Church in the early 1980s, and very soon became the administrative and spiritual center of Russian Orthodoxy. I recently read somewhere that Harvard University saved its original bell, buying it from an American industrialist who wanted to melt it down. The university returned the bell to its rightful owner at the beginning of the twenty-first century.

We could not get out of the hotel, because the taxi driver we called refused to drive us through flooded streets in the dark. There was an uncomfortable scene at the front desk: we were not married and in the middle of the Russian holy place, but Alex could pay cash, and in dollars. The only room available had a single bed. It was available because someone had cancelled a reservation at the last moment.

Alex announced that he could sleep on the floor if they did not have a folding bed. They did not have one—the man at the front desk was smiling. He told us that several princesses were staying in the hotel's best suites. They had come to Moscow before Saint Petersburg's reburial ceremony of the Romanovs, the last Russian tsar's family. We were told that one of their personal assistants got sick before he departed from Europe, so his room was now available to us.

The first night with Alex at the Danilovskaya Hotel, surrounded by Svyato-Danilov Monastery, St. Simeon the Stylite's Gate-Church, Holy Fathers of the Seven Ecumenical Councils Church, Trinity Cathedral, and the official residence of the Patriarch of Moscow and All Russia, felt like a futuristic moment of truth. Perhaps it was a blessing for our union.

We were in a small luxury room with only one very narrow bed. I was looking at it and said, "Alex, I am not sure that I am

ready to take our relationship to the next level—it's too fast for me."

Alex hugged me from behind, sniffing my ear, murmuring into it, "I am not rushing you. You do not need to do anything. And the last thing anyone can blame me for is being fast . . ."

The song "Who Wants to Live Forever" was playing (Alex had brought me the full collection of my favorite rock group's CDs from America, together with the latest model of the Sony compact CD player), while every part of my body was slowly kissed to the point that I could not take it anymore. I never felt so adored or special in my entire life! The lyrics from Freddie Mercury's song were vibrating inside my head—I did not want to live forever and "forever is our today."

I fell asleep comfortably pressed into Alex's body, which was perfectly shaped around me in our bed. In the morning, Alex found me downstairs arguing with another front desk clerk about the breakfast that we had paid for the previous evening. I was told that we could not have our morning meal since only the royals would be served food in the luxurious dining room before leaving for Saint Petersburg.

Ordinary people do not mix well with royals, I guess. When we left the hotel, we saw a line of black cars with a dozen bodyguards who looked like Bratva, Russian mafia soldiers. President Boris Yeltsin was talking to Patriarch Alexy II in front of one of the vehicles.

It was the early morning of July 17, 1998, eighty years since the entire tsar's family with his five kids, Dr. Botkin (the famous Russian doctor who refused to leave the Romanov family on multiple occasions during their imprisonment), and a few of their personal servants were murdered at Ekaterinburg by the

Bolsheviks. There was a special reburial ceremony in Saint Petersburg's Saint Peter and Paul Cathedral that was being attended by more than fifty relatives of the Romanov family from all around the world, President Yeltsin and his wife, many politicians, and other Russian VIPs. I found this rare not staged picture of the tsar's family (without Tsarina) with Dr. Botkin on the left and three of his sons (the youngest one is in the front and the two oldest with a friend are in the back) taken in 1917.

V

"Lara, what did you learn from your past life as a Greek warrior?"

"I realized that I never want to be a military man again! I would like to know how it feels to create beauty."

"Let's have you relax and start counting backward with your eyes closed. Lara, describe what you are seeing now."

. . . I see her for the first time: her inner perfection, goodness, and inborn intelligence shine like gold in the rays of the sun. The commanding power of her personality manifests itself in her striking appearance. Everyone around notices only her physical fairness and is attracted to it like a moth to the light, but not me. And she knows that I can see the real her.

She is drawn to my sensitivity, which regular men do not possess. There is a tense awareness that if I approach her, she will be mine in a biblical sense as well, but she is a married woman. And being a man of honor, I cannot take advantage of her. Her iconic beauty attracts many painters, calling for adoration more than sexual desire. Two brothers from the powerful family can feel it, too, and play their part in making her seen by everyone in our art community.

She teases me, saying that I cannot portray her as well as others have. To prove her wrong, I agree to paint her head only for an upcoming tournament's banner. I depict her as the helmeted Athena, the goddess of victory and wisdom. While she sits for it, she complains about her new shoes being too tight and removes one of them. She has the perfect foot of a Greek goddess: sizeable, beautifully shaped, with the second toe longer than the first one. I am trying ridiculously hard to hide my sensual excitement. Do I have a foot fetish? It is engraved in my mind,

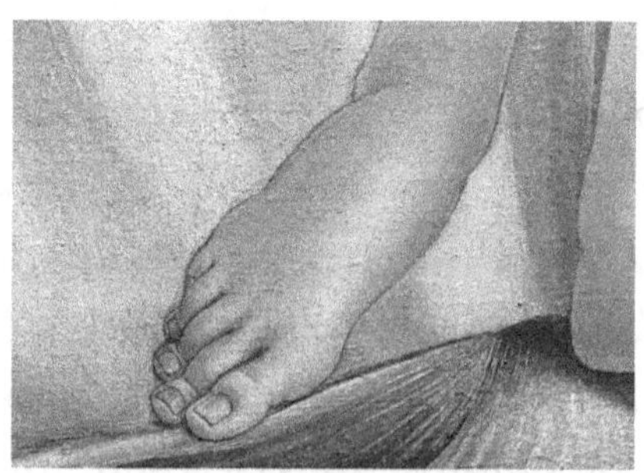

and I will be painting all feet this way for both sexes from now on. (Alex has similarly shaped feet, with high arches and long second toes.)

"Did you meet anyone to love and marry in this life?"

No, and she died too early. Her husband was not worthy of her, and remarried in no time, without a proper grieving period. The only man in that family worth mentioning would be the astrology-driven explorer (the Americas were named after him).

I took full two years to grieve, as a true God-sent husband should, then I started painting her as my Madonna. I employed my dead muse as my model in a lot of compositions, fantasizing how she would look as she grew slightly older and more mature. I chose to wait for a very long time before allowing myself to use her enchanting image as my mythical Venus. I feel so good about deciding to apply a real gold leaf to her hair in my creation. This painting is a final consummation of our union—a fervent but respectful illustration of my timeless adoration for my muse.

"Lara, would you like to add anything or see yourself leaving this life?"

I want to spend an eternity at her feet as a recognition of my undying devotion to her . . . I made her ageless, and she, by her pure existence, made my life fulfilled.

VI

End of July 1998: Budapest trip

I was having a massage at a local spa with a male therapist. In the middle of the session, he asked if I needed anything else for my body.

"Would you like to remove your underwear so we can go deeper?" he asked me. I felt something smooth and wet in my hand.

"I wanted a regular massage only! I never remove my underwear for it!" was my answer, while I was shaking his body part away from me.

"I thought all Russian women are easy and fun," the therapist said, zipping his pants.

I jumped from the massage table, pulling a sheet around my naked body. "Fuck off!" I stormed out of the room.

I was shaking all over with disgust as I got dressed in the women's locker room. I knocked at the spa manager's door.

"Please come in." There were two of them sitting and drinking tea.

"I would like to report an inappropriate behavior of one of your therapists during my treatment," I said, looking straight into the therapist's eyes. He was smirking.

"What inappropriate behavior, dear?" the manager inquired in a syrupy voice.

"This man, coming on to me while performing a massage." I looked at my offender again.

"There were no eyewitnesses, right? And you need to be grateful, not angry, that an attractive man was interested in you," said the spa manager, scanning me from head to foot with a nasty smile.

Red-faced, humiliated, and feeling small, I left the office with my palms curled into fists, hearing the two vile men laughing.

Russian women are spirited, not easy. They are the other way around—they are difficult, intelligent, well-educated, brave, and strong. They NEVER had a choice—they must be brave to survive Russian men!

****

Flashback to my childhood:

My father is taking me home from daycare (I am around five years old) and asks me about my day. I am terribly upset about a new boy picking on me all the time, hitting me hard when nobody looks. Dad stops in the middle of the pavement. "Lara, here, give me your palm. Now, you need to close it into a tight fist. What can we use our fists for?" he asks me.

"We can fight, Papa?"

"That's right, girl! We can fight back."

"But good girls don't fight," I say, feeling confused.

"Listen to me. When someone hits you, you need to stand up for yourself and fight back."

The next day, it is Mom's turn to pick me up.

An angry woman with an upset son is waiting for us at the daycare's exit.

"Hey, your awful daughter attacked my boy today!" The woman is pointing her shaking finger at me.

My mom stops abruptly, still holding my hand, turning me sharply around to face her.

"Lara, is this true?"

"But, Mama, he kicked me first!"

"It doesn't matter who started it. Did you hit this boy?"

"Yes." I shrink away from her; afraid she will slap me in front of them.

"Good girls do not kick other people. They ask for help. Let's go home."

My mother turns to the other woman. "My deepest apologies to you and your son. She will be punished. And it will never happen again."

The boy smiles widely.

****

The next morning, I woke up in bed with Alex tenderly tracing my body with his finger, staring at my butt with bruises left from the massage encounter. "When and where did you get those fingerprints?" he asked.

"Oh, the therapist pushed too hard yesterday. I am easily bruised. It was a great massage, though!" I was trying to keep it light because that spa massage was a present from Alex, and I had grown up in a society where women were blamed for being too provocative.

VII

August 1999

I was meeting with my future mother-in-law in Moscow. She brought a book from Israel for me, signed by her close friend and one of my favorite modern Russian-Jewish poets, Igor Guberman. He had also added a funny sentence about his hope for Lara going easy on Alex. She had a very unusual name—Renata. I heard it for the first time four months before meeting Alex, at a concert in which her beautiful, funny lyrics were used in several songs.

Renata had tickets for a dress rehearsal of the ballet *Don Quixote*, and they were without assigned seats. Upon entering the Bolshoi Theater, we heard an announcement that the orchestra seats were reserved for former ballet dancers, and everyone else needed to go to the balcony.

"Okay, Lara, we should go upstairs," Renata sighed.

I took a step toward the orchestra, keeping my voice down. "And why do we need to go to the balcony?"

"Because we are not ex-ballerinas. At least I am not." She gave me a curious look.

"And who is going to check? I don't believe in blind obedience. You?"

"I will follow you, Lara."

We walked right up to the attendant.

"Ballerinas?" he asked.

"Yes, we were!" I made full eye contact with him.

"Go ahead and take any seats you like."

"Lara, I cannot believe it worked!" Renata exclaimed happily.

Rather than lissome former dancers, the two of us looked like the female version of Cervantes's famous pair. I was the gangly Don Quixote and Alex's mom was Sancho Panza, tiny and slightly plump. We took seats in front of the sound mixing station, where the director of the Bolshoi, Vladimir Vasiliev himself, was chatting with a music engineer.

He was not as famous in the West as Rudolf Nureyev or Mikhail Baryshnikov because he had never left his native country, but his aptitude and talent were on the same level as theirs. His comment on the secret of a long-lasting union with his stage partner and wife that "the man must not get in the way of the woman—she is the most important person on stage," is one of my favorite quotes.

So, there we were, sitting in front of the famous Russian ballet dancer, Mr. Vasiliev—still a striking man at his age. He made a funny observation about "the heavy-for-a-ballerina bottom" of the daughter of a famous Russian comedian after she fell onstage and started fighting with her partner, who had dropped her. She stomped her feet and shouted at this red-faced young man. He looked embarrassed and tried to explain that he had slipped on donkey's poop. Yes, the production had a real horse and donkey that appeared a few times during the performance. Mr. Vasiliev cursed in a low voice the maintenance guy who was in charge of giving enemas to both animals.

Renata thanked me profusely at the end of the evening for the once-in-a-lifetime experience of being so close and overhearing all the comments of the Russian ballet idol of her generation. She was bigger than life herself, famous, and knew a lot of prominent modern authors, actors, and musicians, yet she was too modest to ask anyone for favors. The orchestra during this rehearsal was almost empty, with all the balcony seats taken.

I do not understand why so many former Soviet people's first impulse is to obey the rules, do what they are told, follow the crowd without even thinking about doing something different. Does it have to do with the instilling of obedience in our formal classical education, or our lack of information, or is it in our blood?

As one of my American friends who grew up in Uzbekistan (a former Soviet Republic) said, "We are all products of Mumu's story and the serfdom that ruled in Russia for more than 200 years."

All kids in the USSR grew up with Ivan Turgenev's short story of Gerasim, a deaf and mute serf peasant, who was forced by his strict lady owner to kill his devoted companion dog Mumu (that was the only word he could pronounce) by putting a stone around her neck and drowning her in the river. Until the very last moment, I hoped that he would change his mind and rescue the only creature that truly loved him. How I cried and how I hated Gerasim for this ultimate betrayal of the unconditional love of his dog!

VIII

Another regression therapy session

"Lara, what do you want to discover in your next past life?"

"I want to experience love without a sexual aspect to it."

"Okay, let's try to connect you to the life where you learned to love unconditionally."

I see a forest with a simple house in a clearing. My view is still foggy. I am getting out of a comfortable carriage drawn by two well-bred stallions and driven by one of my servants. I am wearing a fancy black suit with a white shirt and a black bow tie, there is a top hat on my head, my shoes are soft and shiny. I have bushy sideburns, protruding from underneath the hat, and a mustache.

I go inside the hut to pick up a newborn baby. I do not know the sex of the baby, and do not care after losing several of my own children. My wife was stricken with grief and has not been able to have another child, though we have been trying for a long time. An old woman tells me that this baby is healthy and that the mother is a young, beautiful fallen woman who was glad to get rid of it. I give the elder a fat roll of cash before leaving.

Now, I am arriving at a big house with impressive granite columns. My wife's maidservant runs to take the basket with the crying baby from me.

I enter our salon after refreshing myself. My spouse is staring at the new arrival with unblinking eyes full of tears. I want to know the sex of the child now. She is cupping the baby's rosy cheek while unfolding the blanket. It is a girl.

I am a wealthy newspaper owner living in England.

The voice of my mediator interrupts me: "Let's move forward within this life."

. . . We are sitting around a long dining table, celebrating our daughter's fifteenth birthday. She is the apple of my eye. I love her so much that it hurts sometimes. We are tremendously happy. My beautiful wife laughs a lot now. Our dining room is lavish, full of friends making toasts and servants changing dinner courses. Someone starts to play piano, and my daughter ceremoniously invites me for a fast waltz. Then, it is my lovely spouse's turn for a round of stirring gavotte.

"Lara, let's see the end of this life, please."

I am lying in my post bed with heavy maroon curtains. My grownup daughter is holding my hand while trying very hard not to cry. I feel so proud of her. She was one of the first women to go to college, and she passed her exit exam. My spirited girl became an editor at my newspaper, using a fake male surname. She is very taken by the women's emancipation movement. She is not married yet—not for a lack of proposals. I see her from above now, shaking from grief, covering me with a bear hug. I am catching sight of her beautifully shaped long fingers for the last time in this life. She is my Rachel—my biological daughter in my current life.

"Lara, what do you wish to have done differently in this life?"

I did not help the mother of the child I had adopted. I am afraid the young woman was told that her baby did not make it. I think she died from disease or starvation soon after. My ignorance was a mistake.

****

If you knew that by hurting someone or by not helping another human being when it was in your power, you would pay in one of your next lives by having that person as your parent, or your spouse, or even your child, what would you do differently?

I believe that in my current life, that unfortunate woman was my mother. Mom had borderline personality disorder, which made her think that no one could genuinely love her. She fell apart every time I did even the smallest thing not her way, saying that I wanted her to die. I felt like I was walking on eggshells her entire life.

I understand now why she gave away the only pet I ever had in my childhood, a pet I dearly loved—my beautiful tri-colored guinea pig Fomka.

After I came back home from spending two months sick with hepatitis A in a hospital (where I was also infected with hepatitis B through poorly sterilized needles), my mother told me that Fomka died because my disease somehow got transmitted to him. Subconsciously, she made me "pay." I know you cannot compare a baby to a house pet, but try explaining that to a heartbroken eight-year-old girl!

When I was sixteen and my mom was dying from cancer, she apologized for just one thing she had done to me: she had lied about Fomka's death. The truth was that she had given him to her co-worker's family. I asked why she did not get him back after seeing me grieving so badly. Mom answered that the other girl was younger and did not want to give him back, adding, "You were always tough and strong-minded to overcome anything."

Both of my parents died early. They were very unhappy, crushed by the hard Soviet life and mental health problems. They kept trying to break my spirit and my heart daily, piece by piece, with their fears, constant fights, doctrines, physical punishments, and negative views of the world. Sometimes, I feel that the main reason they had to leave so early was to protect me from their unhealthy influence.

They made efforts to love me but did not have the capacity to display it, being on an unconscious mission to get even for the things I had done to them in our previous lives.

IX

September 2001

We were all together, hugging and crying around the large TV screens at Harvard Business School (HBS). We watched the live footage of the burning Twin Towers. There were small human figures on top of them, above the fire. Sheer horror penetrated every cell of my body. "Someone just jumped!" cried a voice in the crowd.

SILENCE, COLD, DEVASTATION, PAIN, HOPELESSNESS, ANGER, DISBELIEF . . .

The world was changed forever by the 9/11 attack, and our wedding plans fell apart. Alex's parents could barely make it to our marriage ceremony on September 21, since most flights had been canceled. We had a wonderfully simple event at Cambridge City Hall. No wedding dress, no gifts, no friends—just two plain gold bands to exchange. There were four of us, and we were content to be alive, in love, and together.

There was a surprise party the next day at a Cambridge bar for Alex and me, planned by his classmates from HBS. It was a shocker to me.

We were coming back from a nice Saturday hike, tired, sweaty, and covered in mud. Alex looked super manly. I had dark spots under the armpits of my gray T-shirt in addition to a red sunburned face.

"Honey, there is a nice bar next to our place. Let's stop by for a drink and appetizers before going home," he suggested.

"I am not sure it's such a good idea," I said. "I am exhausted as well as dirty. I need to shower and change."

"Oh, never change, my love. You are perfect the way you are! And I am famished."

My heart skipped a couple of beats. There was nothing I wouldn't do for this outrageously attractive and intelligent man. We parked our car, then entered the cozy, dimly lit bar.

"Surprise!!!" The sound of many voices drilled my brain.

In seconds, we were surrounded by good-looking, well-dressed young men and women, showering us in con-gratulations and flowers. Alex's entire business school section was there to celebrate us. I was stupefied and unable to breathe, literally feeling like the mobster, who died from a heart attack at the family surprise party, in the movie *Get Shorty*.

Thanking people left and right, keeping my arms glued to my sides for fear of the smell of sweat coming from me, I made it to the small restroom in the back of the establishment. Finally, alone, I locked the door and slid to the floor. I felt ugly, dirty, small . . .

****

Flashback to my childhood:

I am six. I broke my nose on the kindergarten playground a couple of hours earlier. The teachers are upset, trying to figure out who pushed me into the wooden playground column so hard. It is a week before New Year's Eve, and I was chosen for the role of Snow Maiden to give away gifts at the holiday party. They suspect that some girl did it because she was jealous of me.

No one could reach my mother. The doctor comes to apply a couple of stitches without giving me any painkillers. My eyes are badly swollen. I can barely see when Mom appears to pick me up after her office hours. She takes one look at me and sways on her feet, holding the back of a chair. She cries, "Oh my God, who is going to marry her now?"

I am standing right there in the middle of the room, feeling hopeless with my arms hanging open for her hug . . .

A week later, another girl is happily chirping away at the holiday party, wearing the costume made for me. She is announcing kids' names, standing next to Grandpa Frost (the Bolsheviks' substitute for Santa Claus). Humiliated, I try to hide in the back of the room, wearing only a ridiculous colored paper crown I made for myself the night before. The previous day, I was told by one of the teachers that my damaged face would not be suitable for the holiday party's leading role anymore.

****

"Who is going to marry you?" said my inner voice.

"I guess someone just did!" I answered myself.

My train of thought was interrupted by a knock at the restroom door. I must return to Alex's friends. I splashed my face with cold water. I needed a strong drink badly. I had to put a happy smile back on my face. No wedding, and now I would look awful in the photos with the fancy HBS crowd. Somehow, I felt like I was back in time at that New Year's party.

I think that was the first time I sensed that Alex had mistreated me, first by planning poorly, and then by making me pay for his mistake. You should have seen the photos of me with a sunburned face, sweaty, dirty hair plastered to my scalp, standing next to the dressed-up HBS beauties. Very soon, this became a theme of our marriage: Alex's prioritizing the needs of other people at my expense. I was deeply in love and missed all the signs of disappointments to come.

X

We were taking a ferry from Boston to Martha's Vineyard to spend the weekend with two HBS families. One of them was the daughter of a successful businessman, who played a big role in President Clinton's first campaign. She and her husband were generously hosting us in a luxurious villa with a helicopter pad and spectacular views.

At the end of the ferry ride to their place, a tall father was carrying and burping a baby. When he passed me, sitting next to Alex, the baby threw up on my head. This sleep-deprived dad did not even notice and disappeared without apologizing! A couple of kind old women gave me some napkins.

Before I left for the restroom, Alex said, looking at my stunned but smiling face and the stinking mess on my head, "Honey, I think you are ready to be a mom."

"The question is whether you are ready," I wanted to know.

"To be a mom?" he smiled in return.

"No, silly, you are pulling my leg! Are you ready to be a dad?"

"Not yet," was his answer.

Upon arrival, we learned we would be spending the night in the best guest bedroom—the one that had been used by the Clintons. We were surrounded by the framed informal pictures of those two powerful families. I was sitting on the edge of our bed, facing Alex with a naughty smile. "Are you going to do your First Lady, Mr. President?"

"Gladly!"

✶✶✶✶✶✶✶✶✶✶✶✶✶✶✶

August-September 2003

We had moved from Boston to San Francisco for Alex's new job with Genentech, an exciting and innovative biotech company. A good-looking Israeli ex-military intelligence officer named David, one of Alex's schoolmates, was staying with us in a beautiful townhouse in the Marina neighborhood. Our new temporary home, which Genentech rented for us for two months until we could find our own place, had three nicely furnished bedrooms. Alex was working extra hours while I was finishing a couple of online courses for my master's degree and looking for a job. David and I often had nice long talks over breakfast about his struggle to define his new career. He was trying to find a path to professional and personal happiness in America, but his family wanted him to go back to Israel. I felt like I was playing the role of his therapist.

One weekday morning, he entered my bedroom while I was picking up my bra from the shelf, wearing only panties. From the shock of the unexpected intrusion, I dropped the bra on the floor while shyly trying to cover my breasts (or a lack of them) with my palms.

"What happened to knocking?" I asked as I stared at him, using one hand to imitate the tapping move. Even in a moment like this, I could not shake my habit of using my hands when I talked. It had stuck with me from the time my English was basic.

"So sorry, my cell phone died in the middle of a call with my father. He is worried that I still do not have a job offer. May I use your landline, please?" He moved his hand to his heart, imitating the honesty sign, looking deeply into my eyes. He was wearing only pajama bottoms.

My eyes followed his hand first, then moved from his chest to his well-defined abs and back to his daring eyes.

"It's nice to hear that you and your dad are so close."

There was an uncomfortable pause.

"David, please take the phone. And for the love of God, get out of my bedroom."

"Thank you, Lara." He left the room with the phone.

I felt frustrated with myself for the rest of the day for getting aroused.

The next day, Alex and I flew to San Diego, where he had a conference to attend. We stayed at the Hotel Del Coronado, famous for being the filming location for *Some Like It Hot*. We were having a lovely dinner with fine wine, laughing a lot, remembering funny scenes from this movie, and I told him about the previous morning's accident.

Alex shared a Cheshire cat's grin with me. "Does it matter where you get your appetite as long as you eat at home, darling?"

There was no suspicion in his eyes, no anger, no jealousy—just pure love!

XI

Back to September 2023

"Lara, do you want to see more past lives to help you understand your marital challenges better? Let me count down, bear with me. It will take time to make you relax today. Okay?"

Yes . . . I am sitting on a blanket in a beautiful meadow full of people. The scenery is like an Impressionist painting. It is somewhere in France. My two energetic younger brothers are running around with their tired nanny chasing after them.

Our house is spacious and airy, with a lot of paintings. My father is a successful banker and an art collector. He likes the Impressionists, and even made me sit for one of the portraits. It is hanging in our salon to make my father proud, as if my appearance is my main achievement in this life.

He is strict with my brothers, but he adores me. I have the best possible tutors in piano, French literature, the English language, etc. He is very demanding about "lady-like" behavior, though. I am not supposed to speak or laugh loudly; I need to keep the level of my excitement low; I need to listen more while talking less.

"Lara, let us move forward in this life. Can you recognize anyone?"

Yes, I can see clearly now that Alex is my father. I am in love with one of my tutors. I believe he was my high school sweetheart in my current life (he was not sweet on me, though, just one of my friends). Father is very annoyed by this and makes a quick marriage match for me with a son of his rich friend. I feel that Alex is orchestrating my entire life like a conductor. It is suffocating! I cannot shake him off, even after my marriage.

"Lara, let me speed it up. What can you tell me about your last day?"

I am dying from the flu or pneumonia. My father is sitting next to me, holding my hand, and begging me to stay. My obnoxious husband is standing next to him, not overly emotional. The doctor is a few feet away, nervously clutching his dark brown satchel and sadly shaking his head. I can hear the high-pitched voices of my small children behind the closed doors of my luxurious bedroom. My long, heavy, light-chestnut hair is on the pillow, spreading all around my head like a halo. I am asking my maidservant, who applies cold wet towels to my forehead and neck, to cut off my hair. It is choking me. She gives my father a scared look.

I want to break free . . . It is so hot . . . I cannot take it anymore and am leaving my body.

My father (Alex) is shaking my lifeless frame violently, saying that I cannot do this to him.

****

June 2005

We had been at a big teaching hospital for a week when they finally brought a folding bed for Alex. He had been sleeping next to me on three shoved-together chairs, holding my hand. They could finally give me morphine after I lost my second-trimester pregnancy a day ago.

I felt that I had a better chance to make it now, even though sepsis was still in my bloodstream, making my blood vessels leak. As a result, I was dying from dehydration. So, they were pumping IV fluids into my veins night and day, making me swell like a balloon. My kidneys had become overwhelmed and stopped working. I was on dialysis. One of the doctors told me that if I survived, I might have to stay on it for the rest of my life. I was only thirty-six.

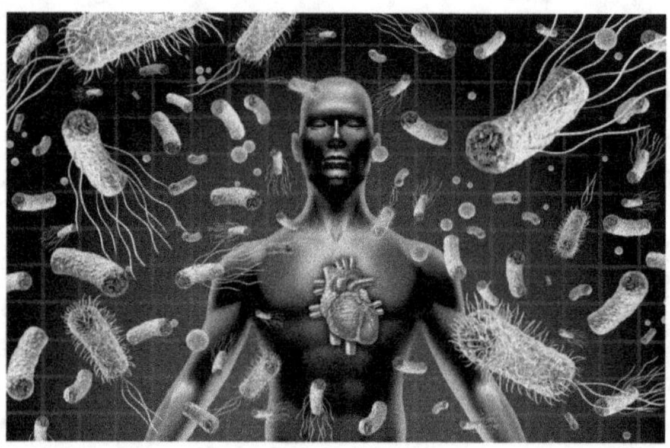

Something was not working again, and they needed to do a blood transfusion. A nurse was putting this process together after laying a chunk of frozen blood on my chest. Alex had left to have a late dinner somewhere. I was telling the nurse that the thing on my chest was too cold—that she needed to move it. She nodded, adding something to my IV line without checking with me. Everything got fuzzy, and in a couple of minutes I was out.

I was flying with angels . . . I was pain-free and ecstatically happy . . . I was soaring to my freedom . . .

Then, bright lights were going through my body, and I was back to my painful existence.

When You Die (written in 2005)

When you die, you will fly,
Soar in a dark tunnel to the radiant light.
Its glow is very warm and inviting.

You will hear the whooshing sounds of many wings,
Somehow, they are just two colors—black and white.
And you need to decide which flock to join for your flight.
It is totally your choice, and you will feel safe making it,
With no judgment attached.
It is a journey over your current life:
You can see again all the places and people you loved,
You can experience all the joys of being a child,
And the pains of growing up.
You can look closely into the dear face of your first love,
You will not be able to embrace him or feel his touch,
But the power of his proximity will break you apart.
At this moment you can decide if you want to come back.
Sometimes this choice is made for you,
When they restart your heart.
The pain of lightning is difficult to describe,
It will shake your entire body, bringing you back on a beam of light.
This experience will change you in so many ways.
And there will be a price attached:
For knowing the pulling magnetism and wisdom of divine power
I cannot describe,
For an arousing touch of feathers of black and white
I cannot describe,
For being so free and happy,
I cannot describe,
For the calming sensation of feeling safe and loved,
But no longer alive in the way we understand existence in this life.

It was morning. I opened my eyes to Alex's angry face. "How could you do something like that to me?" he demanded.

"What did I do to you? And why in God's name am I tied to my bed?" I asked, confused.

"Because you tried to kill yourself!" he insisted.

"I did not! Please untie me right now!" I pleaded.

"Not after what you did last night!"

"What did I do?" I asked.

"You tried to pull all your PICC line ports out of your arm and neck," he said sadly.

"Oh, the nurse overdosed me with morphine, I think," I replied.

"How dare you blame the hospital people who are trying to save your life! You will stay like this for the rest of the day!" He stormed out of the ICU room.

I felt miserable and hopeless. In the beginning, they did not want to give me any painkillers to deal with my pain from a terrible infection because I was pregnant. Now they could dose me with as much morphine as they wanted to, without even checking to see if I needed more or not. I felt like a fly caught in a spider's web made of computers and IV cords connected to my body, tracking, measuring, and dispersing the drugs directly into my bloodstream. I did not feel human anymore!

✳✳✳✳✳✳✳✳✳✳✳✳✳✳✳

August-September 2005

It is difficult to describe this experience; I did not have enough support from Alex after coming back home, because he was going through some stressful leadership changes at Genentech.

In retrospect, I am one hundred percent sure that I am alive because of my Alex. With his four years of medical school in Kharkiv, my husband became a part of the team of doctors and nurses, understanding all the details of my treatments, and making decisions on my behalf. He lived at the hospital with me for the longest eleven weeks of my life.

In the beginning, he did not believe that something had gone terribly wrong. Alex is a very fact-oriented person who lives in his head. The moment he saw my blood pressure of sixty over thirty-five on the paramedic's gadget, he somehow knew that it was up to him to keep me fighting for my life. He held my hand for the next several days without any sleep, tightening his grip every time he felt me slipping away into unconsciousness. Several times I was able to hear him through my foggy brain, chanting, "Darling, please stay with me, stay with me, stay with me . . ."

Everyone at the hospital adored Alex. They would do anything for us; we became their favorite couple. There were so many wonderful doctors as well as nurses supporting us, but I wish they had taken the time to quickly read my constantly changing medical history chart before addressing me. One nurse thought that I was pregnant with triplets (this was after I lost my pregnancy and went from 130 to 210 pounds from the liquid retention), and another assumed that Alex was my son. She said to me, "You are such a lucky woman to have a charming son who truly cares about you!" I asked her to bring me a mirror, then to wash my hair, and give me whitening toothpaste, as well. She was right, by the way; I looked thirty years older after a two-week battle for my life.

To summarize my two-and-a-half-month hospital experience: I had my kidneys and heart restarted, I had to tolerate a catheter and two PICC line portals inside of my body, I had a small chemical factory put through my blood vessels, and a piece of flesh died on my butt. I needed four surgeries to shave all the dead cells from it before they could do a skin graft. The spot on my leg, from which that piece of skin was harvested, would burn like hell for a year. I forgot how to walk, because I was not able to move at all for a month. It is BS when the movies show people waking up from a coma and walking right away—in reality, all your muscle memory is gone! We do not realize how much we move around every day, even without exercising. I had to relearn how to walk with a physical therapist, literally moving my weak legs one step at a time with a walker in front of me for a week.

And after all of that, I was afraid to leave the hospital—I did not want to leave! I developed Stockholm syndrome for that place and for my saviors/tormentors. I added another type of PTSD to my list after all the horrors of this seemingly endless hospital stay. I have had to be in regular cognitive therapy ever since.

I was fighting morphine dependency after coming back home. Sometimes, I felt that my addiction had an identity of its own. It was driving me to become someone else—someone or something very dark and scary that I could not understand or control. I could not live another hour as an incoherent junkie, experiencing strong visual hallucinations. So, I spent my days curled in the fetal position on the sweaty cold sheets, clenching my teeth from the terrible pain in my bones. I got up only to drink, eat my liquid food, clean up my vomit, and shower before Alex came home.

He was very annoyed with my decision to go "cold turkey" instead of "slowly decreasing the dosage," which was the program recommended by my doctors.

My weight dropped from a hundred-twenty to ninety-five pounds from the inability to keep any food down. I had never been this skinny before. My withdrawal took almost three weeks.

XII

2006-2007: Having our miracle—Rachel

After receiving a clean bill of health from my doctors, we jumped on trying to have a baby again since we were not getting any younger and Alex's mom, Renata, was struggling with the return of her cancer—we did not know how much time she had left. Mitya, Alex's half-brother, could not have kids after being drafted to participate in the liquidation of the Chornobyl disaster in 1986. He lived alone in Kharkiv, Ukraine.

I was afraid to be pregnant again, and at the same time afraid of not being able to get pregnant after the disastrous infection. But we were given the miracle of an easy pregnancy, then a pre-planned C-section after so much suffering the previous year. We felt extremely humbled by the magic of parenthood!

Being a mother was so hard. No one told me that it is impossible to stay calm while hearing your OWN baby crying! I do not have enough words to describe the all-consuming love of a mother. It is an out-of-this-world experience, and I'd had a lot of life-changing exposures by then. Alex constantly took photos of baby Rachel with his parents. Finally, we had made them very happy.

We asked our favorite doorman to take a picture of us with Rachel in front of the lobby's Christmas tree, since we did not have the time or energy to buy our own. While taking the photo, he said, looking at our tired faces, "Rachel is so beautiful, so beautiful! She does not look like either of you!"

We started laughing hysterically. Because English was a second language for us as well as for him, we understood that this was intended to be a compliment, that he did not mean to say that both of Rachel's parents were ugly. But it sure sounded like it!

✼✼✼✼✼✼✼✼✼✼✼✼✼✼

When Rachel was nine months old, she still woke us up five to seven times a night to be fed and then cuddled back to sleep. We could barely function from sleep deprivation. We tried to follow advice we found online and in books, but nothing worked with our strong, spirited baby. Alex decided to hire a highly regarded sleep consultant. During the phone interview, she told us that crying time would not be more than ten to fifteen minutes, and that her price would be $400 for teaching us how to deal with Rachel. It was a lot of money for us, but Alex insisted on trying this woman's technique, saying that I could survive ten minutes of *The Crying Game.*

Rachel ended up crying for forty-five minutes while the consultant and Alex were holding my hands, saying that she would stop "any minute now." Alex told me during that torture that he could not have his sleep interrupted anymore, and that if I went to pick up our baby, he would be ready to consider a divorce.

It was FINALLY quiet, and we could tiptoe into her room. Rachel's face was swollen as she lay unconscious in a puddle of her own tears. The wooden rail of her crib had deep bite marks. I hoped that she had not broken any of her pearls, her first beautiful baby teeth, but I was afraid to pick her up to look. I had a dull pain in my chest and difficulty breathing.

The following day, I started to lose my hair. In a month, after losing half of it, I got a short haircut. I also had to start taking antidepressants for the first time in my life because I could not get my baby's wailing out of my head. Every time she was out of my sight, I could hear her crying for me.

✱✱✱✱✱✱✱✱✱✱✱✱✱✱✱

September 2011

I was dressing my constantly moving child for her pre-K classes when she unexpectedly jumped, hitting my lower jaw with her hard head. I saw stars and heard a loud crack. One of my molars was broken in half. My teeth were very weak after malnutrition in my early twenties, during the economic crises in Russia.

I was crying while Rachel hugged me, saying that the tooth fairy would be coming with ten dollars for me (that's right, those fairies have become more generous these days). Anyway, it was about time to spend real money on several good implants.

Alex had booked a room at the Fairmont Hotel in San Francisco to commemorate our 10 years of marriage. We were planning to leave Rachel with her nanny, Maya, and Alex's dad, Papa Vadik. It was our first time leaving her overnight.

"Rachel, Mommy and Daddy are celebrating our anniversary today. See, Dad bought a big, beautiful flower arrangement for me. He has booked a fancy hotel for just one night for the two of us. We will be leaving in a couple of hours, and we will not be taking you with us. So . . ."

"Mommy, who is going to take care of ME?" exclaimed Rachel, with the frustration of a five-year-old.

I was slightly surprised that she was not upset or afraid. "I was getting to that. Maya and Grandpa are staying with you overnight. They have planned a lot of interesting things to do."

"Okay, bye," said Rachel, already turning to run to her grandpa, who was writing his math formulas at our outdoor deck table.

I was brushing my teeth before going to bed in our luxurious hotel room with my temporary dentures lying next to me on the sink when Alex surprised me with an enthusiastic hug from behind. I turned sharply to the side and accidentally swept my ugly plastic denture onto the granite floor, where it shattered into several pieces.

We had just had an amazing time at the gourmet restaurant, eating, drinking, and laughing while planning our next Hawaiian vacation for the week of Thanksgiving. We were looking forward to a great night together without having to worry about whether our child was asleep on the other side of the wall or not. Now, I could not open my mouth without covering it—my mood was gone.

"Honey, I am truly sorry, I did not mean to upset you, and I do not care about your teeth," said Alex.

"But I do! Never mind, let's just watch a movie."

✶✶✶✶✶✶✶✶✶✶✶✶✶✶✶

September-October 2012

I was reliving a happy version of my childhood through my daughter's experiences, hoping I was not overdoing it. Rachel had a lot of energy, so I took her to all kinds of activities like ballet, gymnastics, skating, etc. After all my rejections back in Russia for having an inappropriate bone structure and height, I decided to join my daughter in her skating adventures at the Yerba Buena ice skating rink a year ago.

I felt bad for criticizing her over the previous years about not working hard enough to glide more gracefully. It is really challenging to achieve that effortless look of a professional figure skater! Now, whenever I saw any mother shouting at her child from the bleachers, I went straight to the woman and said, "Have you tried to skate yourself recently? It is not as easy as it looks."

Our skating rink was holding a competition one week before Halloween, so I decided to participate to spice it up. Rachel was using the song "Americano," and I chose "Don't Stop Me Now," sung by my idol—Freddie Mercury. I had to cut the music right before the line "sex machine ready to reload, like an atom bomb," though, because most of the skaters were kids.

What I did not realize was that after the slow beginning, I needed to go fast, or at least try to go with the melody. But there was no stopping me now. Our wonderful Canadian coach Louis was having the time of his life at my expense. For the fast part, he included a lot of sharp arm movements that looked dramatically good on him, but I had to pray to God to help me to memorize all of them, and then try to look at least fifty percent as good as Louis did while executing the routine.

XIII

Everything was falling apart. Alex got pushed out of the most promising startup he had helped to create, because the investors wanted an experienced CEO. Unfortunately, the CEO brought in to replace my husband was so incompetent that he failed to take the company public, even though the technology looked very promising, and the IPO market was hot. Just as this company hit the rocks, an earlier venture Alex co-founded in the energy and materials space was going out of business. Here too, the venture capitalists had replaced Alex with a polished "CEO from Central Casting," with great hair and a dazzling smile, but no idea of how to run a startup. Under Alex's leadership, the company's talented engineers had built the first ever demonstration plant converting natural gas into fuels and chemicals, but the new CEO failed to attract either investors or industry partners. The company ran out of money, went under, and we lost our invested savings.

Alex's current startup was not doing great either. It turned out that the work of academic founders was not solid enough to build a company on. My brave, talented husband was getting depressed, not sleeping well, and losing weight. He was thinking about giving up his startup dream altogether and did not know what else he could do. Meanwhile, I felt that it was up to me to keep us going—so after a four-year break, I returned to work.

By the end of the year, Alex made a radical change. He joined a terrific investment firm, and we got some normality back into our lives, together with financial stability. All these developments were hard on him, though. Gone were the articles in *Forbes* and *The New York Times*, talks at buzzy conferences, fancy dinners with Silicon Valley big wigs and flights on their private jets. He felt that his dream of making it to the top was gone.

Me? I had rubbed shoulders with the fancy crowd only a couple of times, so I did not feel deprived of anything.

＊＊＊＊＊＊＊＊＊＊＊＊＊＊＊

2020-2021: COVID-19 time

Our good boy, Rocky, was very upset in July 2019, when I started disappearing for the whole day. He would sit in front of our entrance door with his sad doggy eyes, blaming me for going back to work. I felt like he was saying to me, "I signed up as an emotional support dog—a companion for you—not as a toy to be left home alone!"

So, when we all got locked in our homes for the COVID-19 quarantine, Rocky could not believe his luck. He would run from one workstation to another, wondering who had time to play with him. He looked forward to the late afternoons because that was when we would take our daily hikes at the different beaches around San Francisco. We had a good excuse to be out before dark: we needed to walk the beast. We started inviting Rachel's friends with their parents to join us from time to time for these remote hikes.

Rocky's favorite place was Fort Funston, which has high sandy bluffs, gorgeous sunsets, and a long, beautiful coastline beach. It goes for miles in both directions and is even open for horseback rides. Our dog loved eating the horse poop pellets; they were full of probiotics and fiber.

Rocky was also super happy with this beach because it had dead birds, and occasionally, if he was really lucky, a big dead sea lion. He would dive into its remains, then roll thoroughly and energetically while I ran to stop this unsightly feat, cursing him loudly to everyone's delight. Good thing we usually had big plastic garbage bags in our car. We started calling them "body bags," because even after rinsing Rocky in the seawater, his wavy ginger fur still had the stinky dead flesh remains stuck in it, mixed with sand. So, the rides home on those occasions were smelly adventures for the whole family, driving with open windows and Rocky wearing a bag.

XIV

February-December 2022

My panic attacks were getting worse after watching the daily news and not being able to sleep through the night. I stayed home for a couple of days, feeling sick to my stomach. I was watching my husband's native city of Kharkiv being shelled by the Russian army in real time. I felt guilty about being half Russian! I grew up watching movies of us fighting German fascists, and now the country of my childhood and youth had become those fascists. They are called "ruscists"—Russian fascists—in a lot of Ukrainian news, written without the capital R now.

We were constantly packing first aid and supplies to send to the Red Cross organizations for the Ukrainian refugees.

We did not know what to do about Mitya. He did not want to leave Kharkiv, despite the heavy bombing.

Conflict — Invasion — War (written at the end of 2022)

It always starts with a disagreement, usually about land,
But you know that.
Then, a fairy tale is created to explain the need for invasion.
This time there is another tyrant's vision to unite two nations:

"Be one under the gun!"
This is how they use propaganda to brainwash the vast country's
mind,
To oil the military machine of death.
The Imperial trigger-happy military went from conflict to
invasion overnight.
This powerful monster with its blood-thirsty generals is so
difficult to stop now,
It takes a long time,
It consumes so many lives,
So many lives on both sides!
Humans who have lost their names, their smiles, their dreams,
their hopes,
Their dignity of proper burial.
They go to the earth before their time—often in mass graves,
Graves where mothers will not be able to find their sons' names.
It takes so much pain, work, and love to create a human life!
I hate all generals who cannot feel the same way,
Whose existence is only for war and nothing more!
They forget that they were young once,
thinking philosophically about
The infinity of light and the meaning of life.
Now they are shelling and mining the cities and towns of Ukraine,
trying to make it their domain.
Those military men are taking another nation's future away!
I hope that all their nasty plans fall apart, and the earth just
swallows them one by one:
By the next week's start,
By the next month's start,
By the next year's start . . .

****

May 2023: an attempt at an adaptation of an epic song and a conflict

I had a big fight with Alex over my idea of using an adaptation of an epic song, accompanied by a video, for a fundraising effort he was organizing for his new best friend in Kharkiv's charity for Ukraine. I think it had something to do with his childhood, his dislike of poetry, and something else that I could not understand yet. His refusal to see what was happening inside of me was breaking my heart. He was gladly but sternly there for me with his constant advice on how things were supposed to be done, how our abilities were limited, and how bad it would make me feel when I failed.

I saw the real Alex for the first time in my life: he needed to dominate me to feel good about himself. He was still that amazing guy I fell in love with. He was talented, intelligent, kind, generous, funny, good-looking, and easygoing with other people, though he was not those things with me anymore. But what I also saw after this conflict was that his dogmas, his limitations, his views, and his knowledge of this world were more important to him than I was. Me? I made him truly uncomfortable.

And I felt like that injured girl again, standing in the middle of an empty room with her arms open for a hug of love and support, and the only person who could give her that relief was saying, "No one will be able to understand you, and no one cares what you think or feel, because you are NO ONE!"

My spark for Alex was dying, causing me a lot of pain. I thought I was falling out of love with him.

THE WHITE CROW (written in June 2023)

I am a white crow,
I was born this way.
My parents were embarrassed of me, scared for me.

Or maybe afraid of me?
They always tried to push me back into the crowd, saying:
"You are not special,
You need to blend in.
You stand out, and you must stop dreaming about . . .
For your own sake, you need to be broken to be a part of this gray flock.
Do not be a white crow!
Don't smile, don't cry, don't dare, don't fly!"
My parents died early and left me with broken wings.
It took forever to heal and to relearn to dream.
One of my friends said:
"You just need to fly away,
There is no way for you to be happy here.
You are the white crow.
You stand out—you cannot blend in with this apathetic crowd.
Get out of this godforsaken land!"
My friends were proud,
Very proud of me.
Now I am out,
But my heart is bleeding for that cursed place,
For the people I knew and left behind.
My heart is bleeding out one drop at a time.
The children of the herd I grew up with are being led to fight and kill.
How can you blame me for not being able to sleep?
Yes, I do know that I am living a dream,
That I need to blend in.
I know, I need to listen more, and talk little or not at all,
Because you do not want people to think less,
Less of me.
You are afraid,
Afraid of being embarrassed of me or for me.
It is like saying again:
"Don't smile, don't cry, don't dare, don't fly."

I do not want to be told,
Told what I can or cannot achieve.
If it does not work for you, I would understand and set you free:
You do not need to change for me!
I did it for you, and I know that it will hurt and will not hold.
I was trying to be a chameleon,
I tried very hard, because I didn't want us to be apart.
But now I am fed up!
You used to make me laugh,
You used to make me forget that I am broken inside.
We hurt people we love,
So, I have had enough—I do not want to be loved.
I am done explaining.
I want to rebuild my wild side to start enjoying my life.
I am The White Crow,
I want to stand out,
I don't want to be a part of ANY crowd.
I want to SMILE,
I want to CRY,
I want to DARE,
I want to FLY!

My nickname at my elementary school was The White Crow for the ways I stood out: my broken beak (nose), my height (taller than most of the other kids), and my frequent challenges to our teachers. I did not like this moniker then, but I love it now, because in some cultures a white crow is considered a symbol of transformation or spiritual awakening. Others view it as an omen or a sign of change.

XV

June-August 2023

Alex's father—Papa Vadik—died peacefully in a nursing home. We did not have any parents left; we were not anyone's children anymore.

We had been dropped by Sony Music after three weeks of negotiations for a one-year limited copyright contract for my adaptation of "The Show Must Go On" to use for Alex's fundraising event. In a month, I wrote my own lyrics with the help of my best friends, who are literature professors and musicians. We found a composer who could use bits of the Ukrainian folk songs to write an original new melody for it.

My Spirit Is Strong/We Fight (written by Clara White and Mark Meritt in 2023)—Shortened

Hey, world can you hear us,
Can you see us?
Listen to us!

Verse 1:
Bombed cities, lost and broken;
Shellshock in our minds,
The bloodlust of a merciless tyrant

And his inhuman crimes!
Can you see the buildings burning?
The smoke turns day to night.
Still, we rise from the ashes
And keep up the fight.
Pre-chorus:
The Empire won't let us be.
We are proud and must be free.

Chorus:
The world I knew is burning and breaking,
But my spirit's strong
And though my hopes are badly shaken
Our fight will go on!
The tyrant's will can never break us;
We can see the dawn.
We know the world will never forsake us,
Our fight will go on!

It was taking a long time for the song to be finished, and we could not post it for Independence Day in Ukraine on August 24. So, I created an adaptation of "America the Beautiful," naming it "Ukraine the Proud," and recorded it on my cell phone with my daughter and her friend singing the new lyrics. Later we went to the recording studio and created a more professional recording to be accompanied by a video showing the hope and pride of the Ukrainian people and the devastation of this war. This time around, the original song was in the public domain, so we did not need to deal with any copyrights. Also, it felt good to use the song, which represents America's victory in the Revolutionary War for independence, as a gift for the nation that is now fighting for its own freedom.

Chorus from UKRAINE THE PROUD:

Ukraine, Ukraine, the proud people's land, may God help you succeed.

Your liberation will be coming soon

For the entire world to see!

I filed for the legal adaptation's copyrights and intended to give my rights to it to a charity that raises money for the medical needs of wounded Ukrainian soldiers.

✸✸✸✸✸✸✸✸✸✸✸✸✸✸✸

September 2023

My regression mediator's soothing voice relaxed me so well, making me feel comfortable and warm inside:

"Lara, let us go with the flow today to see what else you need to discover to bring more clarity into your current life. Can you describe where you are?"

I am standing next to an almost new black Ford that looks like one of the well-maintained antique cars I have seen at the Pebble Beach Concours d'Elegance.

Now, I enter my house, where my family is waiting for me around the dining room table. My wife is a beauty with a short curly bob and kind eyes. Two boys (around seven and nine) are running toward me with their toy cars, eager to tell me about their day. After a nice meal, we all clean the table together. Then, I put a jazz record with my favorite song "Stardust" on a black shiny gramophone and tickle my youngster. We all dance and laugh.

I work on Wall Street as a stock analyst. I am well paid, and we are comfortable, living somewhere in New York state. I was able to trade out all my personal stock positions way before "the selling panic" started and will be staying completely in cash during the next decade.

"Okay, let us move forward in this life to an important moment. What can you see now?"

My grown-up boys are standing in front of us wearing military uniforms. My wife is crying, begging me to do something to keep at least the younger one on the base. They are leaving tomorrow for England . . .

"Lara, let's see your last day now."

I am in the hospital with my older son and his five-year-old daughter. I know that my other boy was killed in World War II. My wife was not able to recover from the loss and died heart-broken the next year.

My middle-aged son is expecting another child coming soon. All of us had a terrible fright the previous month during the Cuban Missile Crisis. It is so hard to understand those ungrateful savage Russians acting like that after all the support they got from us in our joint battle with fascist Germany.

I am looking at my son, who is cupping my hand, and my granddaughter, who is staring up at me closely—I can smell her cotton candy breath just before leaving my body. It is a profoundly peaceful end, and I know that I left them a great house as well as money to enjoy a comfortable life.

"Lara, can you recognize any of them?"

I do not know—I am not sure. There is something about the chess games I often played with the boys during their childhood. My younger son was good at it.

****

October 2023

I had a couple of sleepless nights, processing my past life regression sessions, going through them one by one to answer questions about my quest in this life. In my previous amazingly beautiful lives of comfort, leisure, and achievements, I was able to experience all kinds of love and success. I was kind and generous, I appreciated my good fortune and the people around me, and I viewed myself as caring and empathetic. What was I lacking? I finally saw it. I was not able to feel other people's pain. I think my soul chose all the hardships of this life so that I could learn a true sense of humanity and empathy. My quest in this life is to study the true nature of compassion through a lot of physical and emotional pain . . . and somehow act on it.

We had a family reunion at our weekend house in Vacaville as a memorial service for our Papa Vadik. Everyone was flying in from different places, and three families were bringing young kids. There were a lot of hugs and greetings exchanged. It felt good to spend several days with all of them. I finally understood what people meant when they said that they married into a household; I felt like some of us really were family members before in our previous lives.

For example, I had felt a connection with one of Alex's older nephews from the very first moment we met. I remember that strange sensation more than twenty years ago when we sat together to play chess. I am a terrible chess player, but he patiently reminded me of all the moves, and even tried to lose to make me laugh. In that moment, I knew that I had played this game with him before, and I thought I was going mad. This time around, my realization made it difficult for me to break our embrace.

It is impossible for parents to overcome the loss of a child—it destroys the rest of their lives! The next night there was a deadly Hamas attack in Israel close to Alex's dad's former home in Be'er Sheva. The Ben-Gurion University of Negev, where he was a professor of math for more than fifteen years before retiring, lost close to a hundred people: mostly students and some teachers and staff members. It was a shocking tragedy! I tried to keep myself busy writing, talking to everyone, and playing with the kids instead of thinking of the cruelty and unfairness of this world. It felt like a rising rage that could close my throat and choke me with my own acid. I understand how desperation and bad living conditions could make you hate others, but I cannot comprehend how it led to inflicting so much pain on human beings, especially children and young people.

****

I also spent some time watching my eight-year-old grand-nephew playing with the girls. He is brilliant, funny, handsome, kind, great with our dog, and has ASD (autism spectrum disorder).

And then it hit me: OMG, my Alex is wired the same way! *An Ideal Husband*, who also loves playing *Pygmalion* with me, is living with a light form of autism that is very difficult to detect. How did I not see this before? We both know deep in our hearts that we are soulmates, and that somehow gives him the reassurance that I will stay with him no matter what.

I am totally lost! I do not know yet if I will be able to learn not to overreact to his negativity and his fears of failure. With age, these qualities have become more prominent, especially toward me. I can acknowledge now that it is not his fault; it cannot be changed. But can I, with my sensitivity and emotional intelligence, live with it for the rest of my life? I can finally see, even with my *Eyes Wide Shut*, that my Alex does not have the capacity to love me the way I want to be loved and supported.

****

End of October 2023

After we have been in couples' therapy for a month, we still disagree on everything daily, like we cannot stop rubbing each other the wrong way. I feel that the louder I "knock at Alex's door," the more uncomfortable it makes him feel. Do I have enough strength and wisdom to save our marriage?

At some point, I felt so overwhelmed by Alex's irrational behavior, and it was hurting me so much, that I decided to leave. I packed my suitcase, then went downstairs.

While I was putting my running shoes on, our dog blocked my way out by coming to our front door and starting to ring a handlebell. Rocky does this when he needs to go between his walks. He also hates our wheeled suitcases, because he knows that one of us is leaving, and he needs all of us to stay together. I put my suitcase down to take him out.

Rocky pulled me toward Levi's Plaza with its beautiful fountains flowing over natural stones. Alex and I had spent hours running around them with little Rachel, playing hide and seek and splashing each other. I could hear her happy laugh in my head. I could see her running eagerly into my embrace. And I remembered very clearly the sunny day when we were driving on Embarcadero after her skating lesson, and she won our "Love You More" competition by saying that she loved me

"Infinity, Infinity . . . , and a Palm Tree."

Epilogue

FROM LARA

A lot of loose ends need to be tied up for my story to have closure. The lessons I learned through my past lives have helped me to break free from my childhood trauma, changing my brain chemistry so that I could embrace the world and the freedom of being me, and could feel safe and loved without any limitations or conditions. Isn't this what all of us truly want for ourselves and our families at the end of the day—to feel safe and loved?

Here are a few of the concepts I have discovered on the journey through this lifetime so far:

It is very liberating to stop loving people who hurt you, but it is even more liberating to stop hating them.

I was born in Russia but by now, I have lived half of my life in America. I love my adopted country fully and unquestioningly for embracing me; giving me a sense of safety, fair treatment, respect, education, purpose, fulfillment, appreciation; and for introducing me to the spiritual love that is vibrating inside of me like a flow of positive energy. This said, there is always pain in a corner of my heart and some yearning for that faraway country where I spent thirty years of my life, for my beautiful friends and their amazing kids, for their safety and well-being. They are always in my thoughts.

Now, close your eyes and imagine that in your next life, you will be born among your adversaries—just like I, an American in my previous life, was born in Russia in this one. How does it make you feel? With my current life's parents and my native country, I chose to stop loving them instead of hating them. I am not stating that we need to forgive the tormentors or invaders. All I am saying is that we can stand for what is right and fight against evil better if our minds are not clouded by hatred. Hate, even when righteous, makes it harder to accept the divine presence inside each one of us. It also has the power to destroy us from within.

The finality of death is worth postponing, and the miracle of love is worth waiting for.

I loved my parents and my motherland with all my heart! And yet they broke it, together with my trust, so many times and in so many ways that on several occasions I considered ending my life, because of the unbearable pain they caused me. Then, I was disappointed in my affection and passion for men; I felt used and not worthy. It was only in my late twenties, when I met my soulmate, that I was able to change the way I felt about myself. His love in this life saved me in a different way from our previous lives' encounters.

Happy ending? Not so fast! It is tough to stay true to yourself and preserve your relationship over many years of living together. My idol, Freddie Mercury, was right again, explaining all the challenges of staying in love with your true partner in his song "It's a Hard Life." It is not easy to learn to understand, support, take care of, trust, respect, accept, help, and stand by the person you love till death do you part.

To be loved and understood, you need to learn to love yourself. You are divine art.

I imagine that my broken heart now looks like Kintsugi: a piece of pottery art that Japanese culture celebrates as a representation of flaws and missteps of life. It is a way of bringing an optimistic view of the future: "to stay together and true to yourself" when everything falls apart around you. In my opinion, it gives a new definition to the phrase "heart of gold."

For example, my heart feels like a broken ceramic amphora that was restored with gold bindings, making it into art. I am a masterpiece as a result. We all are—one of a kind; but at the same time, maybe we all are the fragments or sparkles of the Whole/Universe/Infinity/Dark Matter/God. Our life experiences mold us into something new that is more beautiful and exuberant than we were before. They are not supposed to break us beyond repair. This is the main purpose of our reincarnations—to learn and grow through the pains of each life.

All this wisdom has already been voiced many times. By sharing my fable, I wanted to bring it to your attention again, using my ordinary person's imperfect life to prove that:

- *It is very liberating to stop loving, but it is even more liberating to stop hating.*

- *The finality of death is worth postponing, and the miracle of love is worth waiting for.*

- *You are divine art—own it!*

With an infinity of love truly yours,

The White Crow
San Francisco, California
September-December 2023

Acknowledgements

A FIRST-TIME WRITER needs constant support and reassurance, which is exceedingly difficult to find in this competitive and fast-moving world. So, I have only a few people to thank for helping me with this journey:

- ✧ To Sarah Goss, my close friend and an amazing professor of English and writing, for holding my hand, encouraging me to write myself, and making multiple edits to my drafts without changing my style.

- ✧ To Genie, my kind and generous cousin-in-law, for calling me a writer for the first time, and for taking my calls day and night.

- ✧ To Frank J. Padilla, my charismatic neighbor and an Air Force General, for providing thoughtful corrections and for calling my story "an avant-garde work of art."

- ✧ To Jack Canfield, my workshop for writers' coach and a co-author of the *Chicken Soup for the Soul* series, for being supportive and kind to me, and for saying that "my narrative kept him awake."

- ✧ To John Lavack, my healer, for being a source of wisdom, strength, support, and humor in the difficult time of my transformation.

- ✧ To Alex, my husband, for eventually making a space in his heart for my spiritual changes and for helping me to process some parts of my writing.

- ✧ To Rachel, my daughter, for being wonderfully all-American herself and for correcting my grammar.

- ✧ To my entire family by marriage, to all my friends, and to all my therapists in America and around the globe for tolerating, supporting, and loving me unconditionally.

Please check out my books, songs, videos, poetry, etc.: www.clarawhitewriter.com

About the Author

CLARA WHITE is a pen name that came from the nickname that I was given at my elementary school–The White Crow. My classmates gave me this moniker for the ways I stood out: my broken beak (nose), my height (taller than most of the other kids), and my frequent challenges to our teachers. I hated it then, but I love it now, because in some cultures a white crow is considered a symbol of transformation or spiritual awakening.

One day, I will use my books' royalties to launch the reconstruction of a hospital in my husband's native city of Kharkiv, Ukraine. There, we will establish a program to help Ukrainians who live with PTSD after the Russian invasion. My own journey from a victim of childhood and youth trauma to survivor, then ultimately to THRIVER, took two decades of struggle, pain, and therapy. I live vibrantly in San Francisco with my husband, daughter, and dog.

www.ingramcontent.com/pod-product-compliance
Lightning Source LLC
Chambersburg PA
CBHW071214130726
47998CB00002B/747